"WaHoo!"
Elementary

"WaHoo!" Elementary

By Hudson Harrison & Bean

"WaHoo!" Elementary

Copyright © 1999 by Hudson Harrison

Summary: Sixty-four pages of poems, prose and pictures revolving around the elementary school experience.

Library of Congress Catalog Card Number: 97-094603
ISBN 0-9661024-0-1 (reinforced trade edition)

(1. Juvenile Fiction. 2. Poetry. 3. Humor. 4. Nostalgia.
5. Education and Teaching.)

Printing and binding: Horowitz/Rae Book Manufacturers, N.J.

The poems, etc. in this book were written by Hudson Harrison. The illustrations were created by Hudson Harrison & Kristin "Bean Sprout" Greenfelder.

For trade information contact:
Hud House (Creative Properties),
P.O. Box 6462, Grand Rapids, MI. 49502

"Morning Bell"

If you're coming, hurry up!
The morning bell's about to ring-
And it won't wait if someone's late,
Four... Three... Two... One...

"I Wonder?"

I wonder if Washington burped out loud?
    I wonder if Lassie ever meowed?
I wonder if Davy Crockett cried?
    I wonder if Lincoln ever lied?
I wonder if Henry Ford got bored?
    I wonder if Queen Elizabeth snored?
I wonder if Einstein flunked a test?
    I wonder if Caesar was a pest?
I wonder if Elvis flubbed a song?
    I wonder if the Wrights were ever wrong?
I wonder if VanGogh scrawled on walls?
    I wonder if Doc Suess made house calls?
I wonder if King Tut caught a cold?
    I wonder if Bach ever rock & rolled?
I wonder if Vikings bounced on beds?
    I wonder if dinosaurs bumped their heads?
I wonder if Poe played make-believe?
    I wonder if Shakespeare used his sleeve?
I wonder if cave women wore perfume?
    I wonder if Boone had a messy room?
I wonder if they'll wonder about me,
    Once I've gone down in history?
If they do, please make this one thing clear...

-I've done all the things I've wondered here!

"The Meddlesome Mop"

"The Tater Tot Tune"

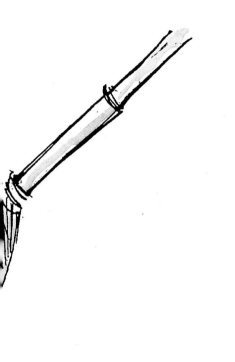

I love hot tater tots!
I'll love them 'til I die.
I love hot tater tots!
And now I'll tell you why.

When you munch hot tots they crunch,
They are the best part of my lunch,
How many do I want? A bunch!
I love hot tater tots!

I love hot tater tots!
Their smell is so divine.
I love hot tater tots!
Don't dare sneak one of mine.

They're soft inside and hard on top,
When dropped in ketchup they "kerplop,"
Once I've started I cannot stop,
I love hot tater tots!

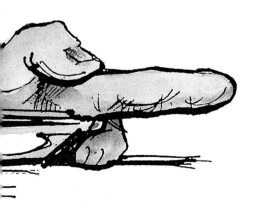

I love hot tater tots!
To me each one is dear.
I love hot tater tots!
Until they disappear.

Parting has been such sweet sorrow,
I can't wait until tomorrow,
Won't someone please let me borrow
Just one hot tater tot?

"Trading Post"

I wish all kids had X-ray eyes
So they could look within,
And see that my true beauty lies
In what's beneath my skin.

But since they don't and therefore won't,
I might as well go shopping,
To find those things I want the most,
Then do a little swapping.

First I'll trade my sense of humor
For Delaney's clothes,
Then I'll trade my love of art
For Lisa's perfect nose.

Next to go is my good nature
For Jenny's golden hair,
And finally, I'll swap my legs
With anyone for theirs!

Let's see... that should be all I need,
Thanks to these trades I made.
Perhaps now I will finally be
The envy of my grade.

What's that? Delaney told my joke
And got a lot of laughs?
Well that's alright, I have nice clothes
And legs with skinny calves.

You say my artwork's on the wall,
But under Lisa's name?
That's a high price for any nose
When my nose worked the same.

And look at Jenny over there
Sharing with my best friend.
No long blonde hair's worth this nightmare,
I want it all to end!

That's right, I said all deals are off!
Here's your stuff in a sack.
And now, if it's alright with you,
I'd like all my stuff back.

I may not have two skinny legs
Or Lisa's perfect nose,
And I may not have hair that's fair
Or wear expensive clothes.

But what I do have are the things
That I value the most,
For these are the things that make me
A very Mary Post!

BY
M.POST

"The Barely Believable Poem of Pink Erasers"

From where do pink erasers come?
They come from outer space.
How else do you think
Some rubber that's pink
Would be able to erase?

In outer space however,
Pink erasers are called "plocks,"
For they can be found
All over the ground,
In space they're as common as rocks.

My only knock against the place
Is nothing is ever erased,
And therefore these "plocks"
Like so many rocks
Just lie around going to waste.

That's not to say in any way
That aliens don't have needs.
One thing they need bad
Is something called "krad,"
(Or otherwise known as weeds).

...And since there's only one place in space
Able to grow such a crop,
They contacted earth
Where "plocks" have some worth
To talk about making a swap.

So now each June a trade is made
Between us and the spacers.
They get enough weeds
To meet all their needs
And we get their pink erasers!

"Thinking Fountain"

What most people don't realize
Is drinking fountains have a brain.
It's not where anyone can see
But somewhere underneath the drain.

What kind of thoughts do faucets have?
I'm sorry, I can't read their minds.
But one thing that I know for sure
Is not all of their thoughts are kind.

For instance, there's one in our school
Where every time you get a drink,
It thinks of some way to be cruel
While your head is in its sink.

One of its favorite things to do
Is to pretend its pipes are dry.
Then when you peek down in its hole,
It tries to squirt you in the eye!

Another is to shoot so high,
Before you have a chance to think,
Its water rains down from the sky,
Causing all your clothes to shrink.

But the most awful thing it does
Is barely dribble droplets out,
Hoping to coax you close enough
To where your mouth will touch its spout.

As you can tell from what I've said,
This is no fountain you can trust.
Therefore, it's "DRINK AT YOUR OWN RISK,"
And hope its "thinker" starts to rust!

"The Creature on the Teacher's Back"

What's that on the teacher's back,
Halfway up and making tracks?
Its body's blue, its tail's black,
That creature on the teacher's back!

What's that on the teacher's back,
Creeping like a maniac,
Searching for a tasty snack?
That creature on the teacher's back!

What's that on the teacher's back,
Crouched and ready to attack?
No one dares give it a "WHACK,"
That creature on the teacher's back!

"Some Words of Wisdom from Mr. Crabapple"
(The school's musty old mascot.)

One hundred and ten years ago, when I was just a baby crab, a student grabbed me from my riverbed and dropped me into this sandbox as a playground pet.

Since that day, thousands of students have come to my sandbox seeking age-old advice in exchange for an apple left outside my hole.

And my advice to you is this...

If, while reading this book, you should see one of my apples in the lower right hand corner, it means the poem is not over and you should turn the page.

Look out, Mr. Crabapple!

DIG!!

Mystery ? Thing!

Step right up, ladies and gents;
The show's about to start.
A show that I should let you know
Will shock the faint of heart.

For what I hold behind my back
Is so strange and grotesque,
It made my teacher yell for help
And hide behind her desk!

I won't tell you just what it is—
For that, you'll have to wait.
But if you want to know the facts,
I'll give them to you straight.

This thing I hold has twenty heads
And forty beady eyes.
Some stare, some blink, a couple wink,
And one pair even cries!

It also has some twenty mouths
An inch or so beneath.
Some smile, some pout, one's tongue sticks out,
And three have missing teeth.

Oh, by the way, did I mention
Each head is in a square?
And that each one's a different shape
With different colored hair?

That's it, that's all the hints you get.
And now folks, if I may,
I'd like to proudly introduce
My weird, wacky display.

A sight so strange and wonderful,
I keep it under glass.
Behold, ladies and gentlemen...

1. "Mr. Blister's Gym Class Rope"

2. "Weird Beard"- It is believed the pirate known as 'Weird Beard' dug for buried treasure on this site in 1695. Though no treasure was found, the holes he dug have filled in to form some of the school's best marble pits.

3. "The Miss Nada Peep Memorial Library"

4. "Ding-Doink"- Forged in 1853 from old pots and pans discarded along the Oregon Trail, this bell's distinctive ring ushered in students for over one hundred years.

5. "Cold Lunch Tables"- Where the school's brown baggers munch their lunch at thirty-two degrees.

6. "The Black Belt Bike Rack"- In its ten years of service, not one tyke has lost a bike.

7. "Thinking Fountain"

8. "Hair-Ye! Hair-Ye!"- On this site in 1989, the lunch lady's hairnet spoke, revealing the secret ingredients to that day's goulash.

9. "Bus #5's Wicked Windows"- Having sprained over two hundred frustrated fingers, this bus's sticky windows were ordered greased by a priest.

10. "The Pink Erasers Drop-Off Sight"

11. "Mary's Missing Molar"- In 1946, Mary Chen's baby tooth popped loose, landing hidden amongst these pearly white stones. In 1997, it was recovered by Eddie "Eagle-Eye" Perez, who placed it under his pillow for a tooth fairy's fortune.

12. "The Glad-I'm-Not-There Chair"

13. "Hide and Go Seek (The Girl Who Peeked)"- It was here that Sally Sneekeroo was caught peeking prior to seeking and banned from the seeker's circle forever.

(14) "Teachers' Lounge De-Bugged"- After flying ninety-five successful spy missions in the teachers' lounge, the 'fly on the wall' was retired with a slap on the back.

(15) "Ooh-La-Lockers"

(16) "Big Green Trees"- They say it was on these very trees that the first tree huggers gave a squeeze.

(17) "Noodle River Rescue"- In 1890, young Mr. Crabapple accidentally floated down this river from the ocean, where he was fished out by an old crawdad who provided him with a cozy riverbed and three warm minnows a day.

(18) "The Peanut Butter Barter of 1972"- The first and only successful liverwurst-for-peanut butter and jelly trade was conducted here in 1972.

(19) "Fun Funnel"- A wind-whistling way to exit the building.

(20) "The 1910 Disciplinary Tower"- Formerly known as 'The Shed of Dread' by unruly students, it now houses a slick slide.

(21) "The 'SPOT' Spot"- In 1887, a stray dog named Spot ate a girl's homework here, giving rise to this age old excuse. Today this excuse lives on, as students claim that Spot haunts the path and eats all their math!

(22) "Noggin Valley Trail"- A shortcut for bus riders willing to test their knowledge in the Whippersnapper Woods.

(23) "Computer Booter Belfry"- According to laptop lore, a computer mouse scurried away from its keyboard here, startling its young user. Two hours later, the youngster lured the plastic pest back to its mousepad with a mega-byte of cheese.

(24) "The Lost Treasure of Teacher-Taken Toys"

(The Pesky Period!)

(25) "The Sally Manella Science Facility"- All blue-flamed Bunsen burners were banned after Johnny Meyer's lab experiment oozed out of control here, resulting in two weeks of extra credit "goop-scooping."

(26) "A Legend Grows"- The mythical monster known as 'Bigfoot & Three Inches' was first sighted in these woods by Mrs. Yikes and her third-grade class.

(27) "Tree of Knowledge"- Pass the test of this old tree and you'll be home by ten past three.

(28) "Knuckle Knocker Hill"- In 1840, a covered wagon carrying the first schoolmarm west of the Rockies became stuck in the mud on this location, which led to the founding of the school.

(29) "The Punctuation Formation"- This ancient stone structure was mysteriously created three thousand years before the first paragraph was punctuated.

(30) "Flunkasaurus"- The skeletal remains of a dinosaur were discovered here on report card day, 1955, by two students attempting to dig their way to China.

(31) "A Twisted Tale"- By sticking a pencil between his toes and spinning like a tornado, legendary children's author "Mr. Twister" spun his first tale here as a child. Ten minutes later he suffered from writer's block, when his teacher, Miss Hayes, made him put on a sock.

(32) "Two Schools of Thought"- On this site in 1997, WaHoo! Elementary defeated its cross town rival, New Century Elementary, in a spelling bee that left the whole town buzzing.

(33) "The Wordstock Festival"- In 1969, thousands of youngsters from across the country gathered in this field to celebrate peace, love, and good reading skills.

131

"Teeter"

Here I sit upon this plank
A boy named Billy Potter,
Hoping to meet someone soon
Before it gets much hotter,
'Cause two seaters aren't very fun
Without a second squatter,
Especially when you're a teeter
Waiting for a totter.

"Daisy May"

She loves me– Yea!
    Daisy May!
She loves me not–
   ...That little snot.
She loves me– Yea!
    Daisy May!
She loves me not–
   ... So let 'er rot!
She loves me– Yea!
    Daisy May!
She loves me not–
   ...That's my last shot!

... She loves me– Yea!
    Daisy May!

(That last one fit back
   In its slot.)

"A Pencil Led Revolt!"

Name: _____

Every student tried to claim
The A+ paper with no name.
It's mine!
Right here!
No, I'm to blame
For the A+ paper with no name!

But though they all tried to claim
The A+ paper with no name,
No one could prove from whom it came,
The A+ paper with no name.

So now it hangs inside a frame,
That A+ paper with no name.
Its fading grade a crying shame,
The A+ paper with no name.

"The 'House of Louse' Hotel"

They don't come by plane,
By train or by boat.
They travel by comb,
By hat and by coat.

Just where they're headed
They don't really care,
As long as it's somewhere
Near somebody's hair.

For hair is the place
Where these little pests
Go on vacation
As unwelcome guests.

They don't pay room fees
Or pick up their keys,
Or care if the sign
Says "NO VACANCIES."

They check in and check out,
Just as they please,
With no reservations
Or apologies.

They couldn't care less how hard you might scrub,
Or how long you rub-a-dub-dub in your tub.

Cleanliness won't affect how long they stay.
You'd wrinkle up before they'd move away!

To get them to leave, what you need to do
Is wash their hotel with *special* shampoo.

Once you've done this, you don't have to worry,
They will start feeling homesick in a hurry!

Nit-pickers!

Then, after they've checked out, take this advice
For keeping these creepers out of your life–

Always think twice before you start sharing
Something that someone else has been wearing.

...But if you do, first make sure that it's clean.
Shampoo that too! –In a washing machine.

Then, once they're gone,
You may begin hugging
All of the students
Those 'buggers' were bugging.

After all,
When it comes
To vacationing lice,
Next time –*your* hair
Could be their paradise!

"Son of Teacher Tells All!"

I'm here today to help promote
the book I wrote last night.
A "kiss and tell" I'd gladly sell
if someone's price were right.

For who's to say what one might pay
to hear a student tell,
the truth about what teachers do
..."After the Final Bell."

What makes me qualified, you ask,
to give you such a scoop?
Well, since I am a teacher's son,
I made the perfect snoop!

So let's get right down to the dirt,
beginning on page four.
This scene takes place, as we embrace,
while greeting at the door.

"On sight my mom gave me a peck,
for which she barely puckered.
My guess was, talking all day long
had made her pucker tuckered."

"She then said she had tests to score,
of which I got a look..."

But to find out what grade you got,
you'll have to buy my book!

And just how well do teachers cook?
That page is a surprise.
But if you wish, I'll gladly dish,
on how they exercise.

"As 'Sweatin' to the Alphabet'
played on our T.V. screen,
Mom never missed a letter
in her whole workout routine."

Alright, that's it! That's all you get!
–Unless you choose to pay.
In which case, to my sad disgrace,
a sequel's on the way!

I'll start it in the morning
after she gets out of bed,
and end it, as the title says,
..."Before Roll Call is Read."

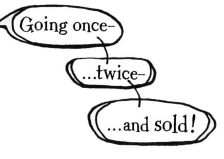

It's a teacher double feature
worth its weight in gold!
You say you'll give me your pet frog?

Going once–

...twice–

...and sold!

"Little Green Kids"

The "Little Green Kids" are coming!
No... They're already here.
Slow down, why are you running?
These kids are not to fear.

They're not green in their color,
They're green in how they act,
And if you care to know the truth
I'll give you all the facts.

"Green Kids" don't fly in saucers
Or live amongst the stars.
"Green Kids" are born right here on earth
And ride in backs of cars.

They're on a lifelong mission
In everyday disguise,
To save the planet they all love
From possible demise.

"Green Kids" love to recycle–
(That's not something they ride),
'Recycle' means they sort their trash.
In this they take great pride.

They also choose to re-use things
And eat what's on their plate.
When it comes to these "Green Kids,"
Waste is one thing they hate!

You say you want to be one?
Well that's easy to do.
Just live your life like these "Green Kids,"
And you're a "Green Kid" too!

"Crayon Daisies / Crayon Crazies"

Crayon Daisies are guys and gals
Who treat their crayons like their pals.
    Crayon Crazies are maniacs
    Who have it in for colored wax.

Crayon Daisies keep a supply
Of every crayon you can buy.
    Crayon Crazies like to borrow,
    Hoping you'll forget tomorrow.

Crayon Daisies stay in the lines
And neatly color their designs.
    Crayon Crazies use the wrong end
    And love to see how far they bend.

Crayon Daisies keep theirs in rows,
In the order a rainbow goes.
    Crayon Crazies don't use a box,
    They just stuff theirs down their socks.

Crayon Daisies, as you can tell,
Take pride in treating crayons well.
    Crayon Crazies, as you might think,
    Would rather see them all extinct.

"Louise LaCheese"

Oh no! Look out! Louise LaCheese
Is on one of her dancing sprees.
She spins! She twirls! She kicks! She whirls!
That girl's Louise LaCheese!

There's only one Louise LaCheese,
On that point everyone agrees.
She's hip! She's cool! She's no one's fool
In school! Louise LaCheese.

And Oh, that hair! Louise LaCheese,
It changes colors like the trees.
First blonde! Then black! Then red! Then back
To black! Louise LaCheese.

But when they tease Louise LaCheese,
Louise makes no apologies.
I'm weird! I'm rare! I'm truth and dare!
So there! Louise LaCheese.

THE ORIGIN OF... "ERASER BOY!"

HAVING BEEN FALSELY ACCUSED OF BREAKING THE "NO TALKING" RULE,

...BILLY LIPLOCK WAS REQUIRED TO CLEAN BLACKBOARDS AFTER SCHOOL.

WHAT BILLY DID NOT REALIZE, WAS AS HE WIPED EACH BLACKBOARD CLEAN, CHALKDUST WAS LODGING UP HIS NAILS, GRANTING HIM POWERS SELDOM SEEN!

AFTER ERASING EVERY BOARD, BILLY GAVE HIS WIPERS A WHACK!

... PRODUCING A THICK CLOUD OF DUST THAT MADE THE YOUNG BOY START TO HACK.

BUT ONCE THE DUST HAD CLEARED AWAY, WHO EMERGED WAS NO THIRD GRADER,

"A Friend Under My Desk"

For reasons of which I'm not sure,
I stuck my hand under my desk,
And felt around until I found
A clump of something quite grotesque.

It was sticky, wet and icky,
And sent cold shivers down my spine.
I wasn't sure just what it was,
I just knew that it wasn't mine.

The simple thought of touching it
Would make most other children squeal.
But no matter how hard I tried,
I couldn't resist one more feel.

First I smeared it to the left,
Then I smudged it to the right.
Anything that feels this weird
Must make an even weirder sight!

But I can't bring myself to look,
The mystery is half the thrill.
Besides that, if I were to peek,
The sight of it might make me ill.

Unfortunately, the next day,
For reasons I can't understand,
My friend was nowhere to be found.

(I think that I'll go wash my hand!)

"Ooh–La–Lockers"

These lockers put on
    Fashion shows
With all the students'
    Hanging clothes.
When do they do it?
    No one knows,
Since no one's there
    To see them pose.

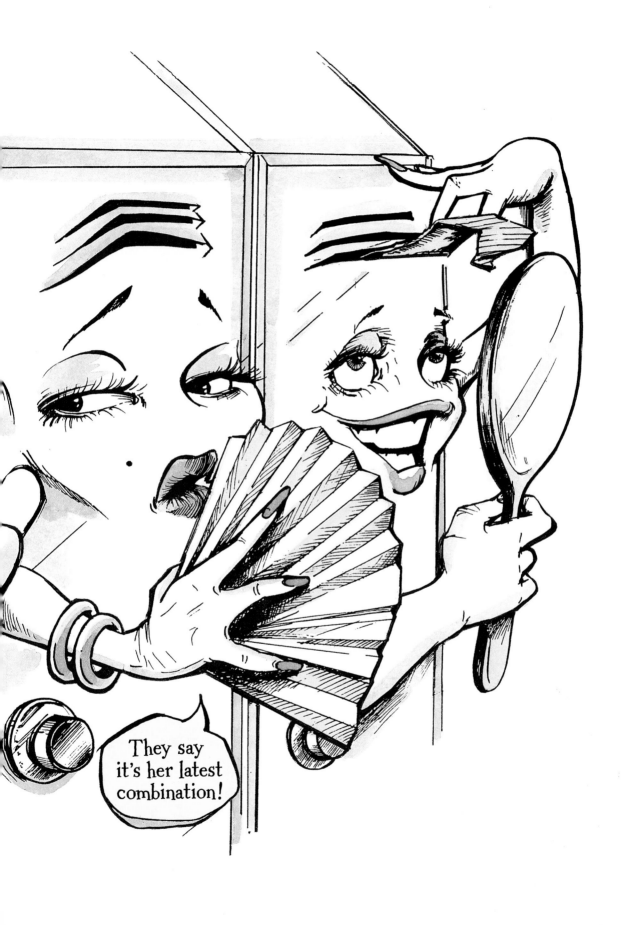

"Tardy Marty's Birthday Party"

Once there was a boy named Marty,
Who was known for being late.
Every day he came in tardy,
Every day his class would wait.
Then one day they threw a party,
Knowing Marty would turn eight.
But this time when he was tardy
They decided not to wait.

First they ate his birthday cake.
Then they sang his birthday song.
Then they opened all his gifts
And played with them all morning long.
'Party-hearty' they all did,
Until they could party no more,
Ending Marty's birthday party
Just as he came through the door.

Not a candle was left standing,
Nor a sip of soda spared.
Every tummy was expanding
With the yummies they had shared.
Only Marty's tardy tummy
Had missed out by being late,
Causing him to feel as crummy
As the crumbs left on his plate.

But wait! Before you seal his fate,
You should know Marty's changed his ways.
The boy once known for being late,
Has left behind his tardy days.
Instead, he rises with the sun
Like any early bird would do,
'Cause Marty's learned it's much more fun
To have your cake and eat it too!

Special thanks to:	GRADE	1st WEEK					2nd WEEK				
		M	T	W	T	F	M	T	W	T	F
1. Baird, Nick											
2. Cappozzoli, Holly											
3. Carter, Jordan											
4. Charminglocker, Michelle											
5. Gareau, Hannah											
6. Gianakura, Pete & Georgia											
7. Greenfelder Rich & LuAnn											
8. Harrison, Charlotte											
9. Harrison, Christian											
10. Jabaay, Jake											
11. Jacobs, Connor & Megan											
12. Jerome, Elyse & Meredith											
13. Kooiman, M.J.											
14. Leahy, Zack & Noah											
15. Mailand, Jim											
16. McMonagle, Al											
17. Melinda, Emily											
18. Niswonger, Laura											
19. Pawson, Cole											
20. Petersen, Jan											
21. Robert, J. Harrison											
22. Schneider, Cassie											
23. Scissorwhiz, Lisa											
24. Scott, Joy											
25. Watkins, Elven											

Teacher _____ Grade _____

Teacher _____ Grade _____

TITLE	PAGE			1st WEEK					2nd WEEK				
				M	T	W	T	F	M	T	W	T	F
1. Barely Believable Poem of Pink Erasers	1	8											
2. Bobbie Jo Backtracker	2	8											
3. Crayon Daisies/Crayon Crazies	5	0											
4. Creature on the Teacher's Back	2	2											
5. Daisy May	3	3											
6. Eraser Boy	5	4											
7. Fly on the Wall in the Teachers' Lounge	2	7											
8. Friend Under My Desk	5	6											
9. House of Louse Hotel	3	8											
10. I Wonder	1	0											
11. Little Green Kids	4	8											
12. Louise LaCheese	5	2											
13. Meddlesome Mop	1	2											
14. Morning Bell	8												
15. Mr. Crabapple	2	3											
16. Mystery Thing	2	5											
17. Name_____	3	6											
18. Ooh-La-Lockers	5	8											
19. Pencil Led Revolt	3	4											
20. Son of Teacher Tells All!	4	4											
21. Tardy Marty's Birthday Party	6	0											
22. Tater Tot Tune	1	4											
23. Teeter	3	2											
24. Thinking Fountain	2	0											
25. Trading Post	1	6											

Period.